G000081433

THE YEAR I MARRIED

BY FILIPPO AKI PIGNATELLI

A classic comedy by a very young author

For Alice Orlando

FILIPPO AKI PIGNATELLI

PROLOGUE

I have always wanted to marry.

My old husband was a movie maker.

I am not like him.

I, on the other hand, am a costume designer.

My old husband was 2 meters high, had brown hair and blue eyes and had peachy skin.

My 2nd husband was an artist, but he was too naughty.

So 1 year later I asked my mum, "Mummy, do you know anyone I could marry?"

She replied, "No, Amy. I don't. Why?"

"For a husband, mummy."

All I really wanted to be was a psychiatrist, but my mum made me be a costume designer.

At first I thought that was a great idea, but I was wrong.

And do you know why I thought that was a great idea? Because in my times, it was simple.

But now it is a nightmare.

I know that it was going to end differently for all the costume designers, but not how I expected it.

The first time, I thought mum had put me in her science lab (my mum is a scientist) to get better at science.

The last time I went to school for a science test, I got F-!!! And that is why I thought that my mum was going to tell me that.

But this is not about my mum, this is about me.

My name is Amy Madigan, I am twenty years old and my mission is to find the right husband!!!

CHAPTER 1
MY FAMILY & FRIENDS

Before we start, I will introduce my friends to you.

My first friend is Anna. She is French, she has blond hair, she has brown eyes, she has round glasses and wears the same pink dress every day.

My second friend is a robot I made in high school. His name is Rover.

My third friend is Mary. She has blue eyes and has a peaceful accent.

And my last friend is Dick. He has brown trousers and brown eyes, short blond hair, a brown bow tie, a peachy jacket, a striped brown and green and white shirt, a gold chain and very light skin.

My mum is very young (45 years) and is very protective on me.

On the other hand, my dad is very cheeky and is always busy.

And now that you know everyone in this book, I can tell you all about me and how I got a lovely husband.

CHAPTER 2
THE GARDEN

One Friday morning, I was going to daddy for a cup of tea. I was 3 meters away when I saw a crowd all around Mr. Loretta's house (he lives in daddy's street).

The crowd kept shouting, "Tell us about your garden!" and "Tell us about the dandelions!"
And even worst half Paris' people were blocking the street!

I saw Dick coming out of the crowd.

I scrambled to him and held his shoulder for support.

When I got there I asked, "What's going on?"

"Mr. Loretta's garden is what's going on," he responded, "Only for its beauty."

It took us two long minutes to get through the crowd.

Dick accompanied me to my dad and then he went home.

Dad asked me the same thing he always asks me, "How are you, Anne?"

"Dad! It's AMY!!!"

I sat at my dad's for a while and then I went.

When I went back home I went to see Mr. Loretta's garden.

And, I have to admit, it was the best garden I have ever seen.

Then I remembered that there was a garden competition and he might have entered.

The prize was £1000.99 and if you were American, it would be $1000.999!

Mr. Loretta is very poor so that was figured out.

Suddenly, Mrs. Loretta came running out of the front door shouting, "We Won!!! We Won!!!"

I ran back home to say everything that happened to mum, Rover, Dick, Mary & Anna.

CHAPTER 3
ROBERT & GORDON

It was midnight. Suddenly, the window opened. Dick came in. "Rise & shine, Amy. Its nine o'clock in the morning!!!" said Dick, cheekily.

I responded lazily, "Five more minutes, mum."

"Amy, it's me, Dick. I think I found the right husband!"

I opened my eyes wider than ever.

I raced past him and jumped out of the window.

"Amy this is Robert!" said Dick.

He was pointing down to a movie maker that was tall as a ten year old child.

I told Dick that Robert was not the right husband.

We stood there complaining and giving reasons to say

that Robert was good and not good.

Surly enough, I won & Dick told Robert that I didn't

want to marry him.

On Saturday, it was worst than the day before!

"What about a French person like Gordon?" Dick said, reluctantly pointing at someone I barely knew.

I slapped my head harder than ever.

"Good morning, lady!" he was saying.

He held my hand and kissed it.

I pulled my hand of his dirty hands.

I was filled with anger.

I was so angry that my face went red.

The two of them ran so fast that you couldn't see them.

I clapped my hands and walked off.

CHAPTER 4
THE INTRUDENCE

That night it was so cold that half Paris was frozen.

I couldn't bear the cold of night.

I was hugging myself for warmth.

When I got home, I rushed to the fire so I could undo the ice around me.

I went to see if it was still there.

And surly enough, it was.

Something is wrong I thought.

I went to find a book to read.

I heard tip-toes at the end of the hall.

I called the police, but spoke in a very silent voice.

I said that some of the biggest thieves that police still haven't captured was in my house.

And you know what? I was right!!!

Bobby Silence (the fattest thief) and Sam Steal (the thinnest thief) were in my house!

Suddenly, Bobby Silence tripped on the broken, wooden path and tumbled right on top of Sam Steal.

The cops came in to take the two thieves away.

I spun around to see if the biggest diamond in the world (that the queen gave me) was still there.

It was!

Dick came running to me.

"What happened?" he asked in panic, holding his knees and looking at me.

"An attack," I explained.

"By who?"

"Bobby Silence & Sam Steal."

Dick ran down to the police car as fast as he could only to see them.

But the car was already gone.

He was pail with disappointment.

CHAPTER 5

STRANGE MEETING

It was a day that I hadn't seen mum so, eventually, I went to visit her at 6 o'clock in the afternoon. As I went, I saw someone in a black cloak, a large American hat and a carnival mask.

"Be careful to who you trust," it says.

A second I think it's a poet, and the other a writer. But mostly a poet. It's as if it was holding me, but it was a dirty little rat.

"The land is like the sea," it continues, **"There is no place like home."**

I saw Dick walking by.

I ran to him, trying to get the rats dirty hand off my shoulder.

Before I can run out into daylight, the figure grips me.

He told me not to say anything.

I promised and he kicked me out of the shadows.

It was dark so I went home with Dick.

CHAPTER 6

POLICE

On Monday morning, I went to get the daily news at the Paris news stand.

It was hotter than yesterday.

As hot as 25^0 of hot sun.

Actually, even hotter!

It was so hot I could barely look at the sun.

The daily news said that at the country prison Sam Steal and Bobby Silence had escaped from jail!

And even worst they locked every single police officer in Paris in their cell!

The first thing I did was rushing to the police so I could set them free to recapture Sam Steal and Bobby Silence.

The second thing I did was running home so I could keep the diamond safe.

The only place was at the bottom drawer.

Then I told Mary and Anna to make a news story of staying alert that Sam Steal and Bobby Silence were on the loose.

And I have to be honest, they did a pretty good job.

When I told Dick, he zoomed to his cupboard, dressed up as a tourist and had a camera in his hand.

Then he rushed back to me and asked, "Where are they?"

I slapped my head and answered, "I don't know."

Then I rushed to my house and I found the sheets from the daily news flying away.

I had lost my only evidence.

I slapped my head even harder.

CHAPTER 7

NEWSPAPER

The newspaper said: "Lock your doors everyone. Sam Steal and Bobby Silence are back in action; for they have escaped jail. Do we have to wait 22 more catastrophic years for them to be captured? Is the police concentrating? Sam Steal and Bobby Silence say 44 more years. Are they correct? Are we going to survive these years? Or are we going to let these two criminals take over Paris? We have to wait and see. It is up to us to protect our children and ourselves. Find out more on

https://www.thedailynewspaper.com."

I hold the newspaper down and looked at my friends.

"This is extraordinary!!!" I said.

Mary and Anna smiled in glee.

"It was Anna's great idea," presented Mary.

I have to say, the two of them are a great couple in newspapers.

I turn around to Dick.

He had a big smile.

Suddenly, his smile faded and he pointed at Mary and Anna.

I spun around and see that they were fighting.

I don't know why so don't ask me.

"I think that it's about who is going to copy it," whispered Dick, clutching his hands around my ear.

CHAPTER 8
DISCUSSION

Soon, Rover came.

I pushed through Anna and Mary.

"**I** want to copy it!!!" said Mary.

"No, **I** want to copy it!!!"

"**Seriously? Beep!**" said Rover.

Dick pushed through us.

"Stop, everybody, just stop," he was saying, "If you two can't figure out who should do it, then I will!"

He took Rover and walked home.

I backed away from Mary and Anna shaking my head.

After, I found Rover and Dick.

I thought about Mary and Anna.

" Dick, are Anna and Mary OK?"

"Of course. Just fighting!"

It wasn't long that I found mum in the street.

I ran over to her, pulling Dick behind me.

"Mum," I said, "Do you mind if I bring my friend, Dick, at 3:00 for some milk?"

"No, I don't mind," she said.

I smiled at Dick.

He seemed to be a little frustrated. So I told him that mum is like any other mum and that did the trick. I have to admit it, but Dick is always scared about going out.

CHAPTER 9
MUM'S HOUSE

I told Dick about mum's house.

Wait, why are you all scratching your heads?

Oh, OK, I see your point.

My mum has a very big house.

The table blanket is white, the walls are grey, a big piano is downstairs, there is a very clean basement, a big library, a little kitchen and a lovely bed.

The thing that disturbs me is my little brother, Fred.

He's calling me "Angel".

I know it's a name that is of an angel, but it bugs me.

Even because he says it as "g" not "j". Mom now knows that I never come the

day I said, but I come a week or a day after.

It is usually because of my work.

She says it is better that way.

And tomorrow, is when I work.

CHAPTER 10
COSTUME DESIGNER

Remember when I said I was a costume designer? Well, that is my chore for today. And that also means no friends around.

Today, I created a Christmas jumper, because in 2 days, it will be Christmas.

The jumper was dark blue, snow was coming down and it had Rudolph the red nose reindeer.

Really, it is for eight-year-olds.

The worst part is, it took me <u>9</u> long hours!!!

And 59 minutes!!!

And 59 seconds!!!

<u>And</u> 59 moments!!!

That jumper was a nightmare!!!

When I went home, I was thinking of going to Dick's.

But, since I didn't want to disturb Dick, I thought I should go and see him tomorrow.

And if the costume company doesn't shut down by tomorrow, I wouldn't have gone to Dick and mum.

CHAPTER 11
COSTUME COMPANY

Usually, the company I work in, shuts down today.

I think that there was a delay, because it didn't shut down.

I pushed to the front of the crowd of costume designers.

When I did, I rushed in the costume company.

"What is going on, Mrs. May?" I asked, clasping my hands on the table and looking at her.

"There has been a little delay," she said keeping her teeth together and staring at me; her eyes wider than ever.

"What kind of delay?"

"We couldn't make any copies of the costumes," she gnarled.

I thought that the company could have done that after Christmas.

"Can't we wait until Christmas is over?" I asked, confused.

"No, we have a lot of circumstances that still have to be sold for Christmas."

Then I realized I had one of the things that she needed.

I ran home and got the costume copier and ran back to the company, so I could give it to Mrs. May.

She said thank you.

Then she let me go.

CHAPTER 12

CHRISTMAS

It was Christmas and I went to pick up Dick.

When we got to mum, she had a big, friendly smile on her face.

She hugged me and Dick and she said, "Happy Christmas!!!"

She settled us on the living room table.

She brought some milk for me and Dick.

"How was work?"

I mumbled, "Good."

We sat there for about an hour or so.

I gave mum, Dick and dad a present.

For mum a mug, for dad a bunch of clothes and for Dick a long hat.

Dick gave me a bushy winter hat, he gave dad a jug and gave mum a pen.

Mum gave me a folder of the family history, she gave dad a plant and Dick a giant dictionary.

Dad gave me a wallet, he gave Dick a picture of me and he gave mum a new potion.

I have to be honest, I thought that it was just slime and water, and, surly enough, I was right .

After I went to the CMTV*.

It was not a long meeting, but it worked for me.

*Christmas Meeting Together at 5:00

CHAPTER 13

THE HAUNTED HOUSE OF JAMES

I started a new book named "The haunted house of James".

I will read you some of it:

"Cold was the night, Linda and James couldn't feel their hands. It was raining hailstones, there were icicles everywhere.

James turned the key to his house door, "Seriously, Linda. Why did you estimate and not look at your phone?"

"I didn't estimate. The phone said so," Linda complained, " Look for yourself."

James looked on his phone.

"Golly! You're right!" James explained.

"Seriously," said Tom the cat.

The three of them fought through the door. They found a game.

"James, did you order a game, or did you?" said Tom.

"No, Tom. I didn't," James answered.

"Well, let's play it," Linda said. They opened the top of the game.

"What," said James, "Where's the inside?"

He looked at Linda. She was looking up astonished.

"Linda what's wrong?"
"LOOK OUT," she screamed.

James turned around. He was terrified. He had seen an enormous vampire!

"AHHHHHHHHHHHHHH," they screamed.

The two of them ran out of the house followed by Tom.

"GOLLY!" panted James." That is the end of chapter one and this book was written by Filippo Aki Pignatelli.

CHAPTER 14
VISITING MARY & ANNA

The next day, I went to visit Mary and Anna.

They opened the door.

I forgot I brought Rover, but he managed to get in, right before the door slammed.

"Hi, how are you?" I asked.

"Good," they mumbled, "What about you?"

"I've been better," I said.

I sat there a long time, talking about the delays.

They were not listening.

(I knew, because they were only saying yes to everything I said).

When I was done, I sat up and walked out the front door.

"Have a good day," I said.

"And you too," they responded.

I thought for a long time if I could ask them for some

advice on who to marry, because I was running out of ideas.

CHAPTER 15

PAINTER

That morning, Dick was finishing some morning accounts.

When he saw me, he had a painter behind him.

He smiled.

"This is Bobby and he is a 29 year old painter," He said.

"Bounjour, madame," he said in a French accent.

Sure enough, he was French.

He was just about to kiss me when I screamed and pulled my hand off.

He turned around to see why I screamed.

That gave me a chance to run away from him.

I don't know why but he ran too.

I saw a spider so then, I knew why he had ran with me.

I laughed so hard.

I never laughed so hard in my life.

CHAPTER 16

SPIDER

I went to the spider with my eyes closed, facing Dick and the painter, and laughing. Then I tried to pull it off.

It wouldn't budge from its spot.

At the same time, I stopped laughing and opened my eyes.

Then after a second or two I turned around.

It was still there.

I asked the boys for some help.

Dick came before the artist, because he wouldn't budge.

We tried and tried, but the spider would not budge.

It was there, not moving a single leg, always in the same position.

We were beside the Loretta's house.

Then I noticed that Mrs. Loretta was coming out.

She had a cutting knife in her hand.

When she saw us she asked us, "What are you doing with our Halloween spider?"

Then I realised that is why the artist wouldn't budge.

Well, he could have told us.

But I guess that he was too shy to tell us that was a Halloween spider.

I thought that it was real because he ran away from the spider.

Mrs. Loretta went away with the spider.

And the artist went away laughing at us.

Dick was looking at me with one of those questions inside and one of the question was "what now?".

I said that we could just do nothing when suddenly Mary, Anna and Rover came running to us.

CHAPTER 17
THE EIFFEL TOWER

"Amy, Amy," they were panting, "the Eiffel tower opened a new romantic restaurant!"

I read the newspaper.

It said, "Napoleon has declared that all citizens that need to marry should have a private place where to kiss. It is a restaurant that is very high, so it would be best a normal restaurant otherwise."

I thought about it for a long time.

It ended up as a no.

Also because I don't trust Napoleon any more after he was emperor.

He wasn't very trust looking anyway.

All hope was lost but at least there was another place

romantic enough.

"*L'amour de Paris*" was the name.

I always passed those streets and everyone was

there kissing.

The first time I thought that they were pretending;

turns out I was wrong.

That night, I went to see the lights of the Eiffel Tower.

There were millions of people in the restaurant.

They must be having fun I thought.

CHAPTER 18

SNOW

The next morning, when I woke up, I went to the window to see the nature.

But all I could see was snow, endless snow.

I couldn't stand the snow so I called Dick to see if this was supposed to be the weather.

But when I connected, the signal was lost.

I went to see it on my phone, but all I could do was wait till tomorrow, because the snow was so hard, you can hardly even work.

Then, I thought that I could just see mom, but there was a blizzard. I could draw so I did that.

The picture was of a girl (me) sitting at her window and was looking at the strong blizzard outside.

I am very good at drawing and I hope

you appreciate my drawing.

It is very messy with rubber, but you

can see me looking outside at the darkness of

the snow crumbling down from the clouds of the

sky. It didn't take me long, because it is only draw-ing

me and window filled with snow.

It really took me 5 minutes to make it.

I thought that it would be nice to make a picture of the nature so it could be like being close to some animals that's all.

CHAPTER 19

THINK

The next day, I thought of who I could marry.

I thought and thought and thought and thought, until 3:00 p.m.

I thought about Dick, he had helped me a lot, he helped find the right husband, he tried.

So I thought that I could marry him...

...well maybe.

He could just be the right one.

He also helped me in English.

When I was alone, he helped.

He still does now, helping me.

He also helped me...

Wait, we can't stay here talking about him forever.

Well if we have time.

But no, so let's go and find out what happens in chapter 20!!!

CHAPTER 20

DICK

The next day, Dick was going to come to me at 2:00 p.m.

So 5 minutes before I sneaked to his house.

When he opened the door, he screamed.

"Dick, I need to tell you something."

"What!"

I cupped my hands around his ear and whispered, "Would you like to marry me?!"

He blinked at me with a smile.

That usually means yes.

I was filled with happiness and jumping up and down.

I breathed inside.

Dick accompanied me home.

He was holding my shoulder.

When I got home, I told Rover.

His sad smile turned in a happy smile.

"Great!!! Beep, Beepity Beep!!!" he said very happily in a lot of glee.

CHAPTER 21

PRIEST

I went to a church named St. Andrews Church.

There was a priest that was not the one I wanted.

Then, I went to a church named St. Pauls church.

There was the best priest.

His name was Father Andrew.

He was a fun priest.

Really, the marrying zone was in a park not far away.

It's a few blocks from our houses.

Meanwhile, Sam and Bobby were in town, about to come in Mary and Anna's house.

They had just come in.

They went in their room...

"STOP RIGHT THERE, BOBBY SILENCE AND SAM STEAL!!!" officers yelled, "YOU TWO CRIMINALS HAVE A DOUBLE DOOR TO YOUR CELL!!!"

They were pail and growling.

CHAPTER 22

MARRYING

The next day, it was the day we married.

There was Rover, Mary, Anna, Mum, Dad, my family and Dick's family.

Oh, it's starting.

"Amy, would you like to marry Dick?" asked the priest.

"Yes," I said.

"Dick would you like to marry Amy?" asked the priest.

"Yes." We kissed.

The park was filled with cheers.

There were whistles and cheers and hat throwing and also hugging.

CHAPTER 23

DANCE

One of my favourite music was put on (Swan lake).

First me and Dick did the waltz, Viennese waltz, tango, quickstep and the foxtrot.

Then we did the Latin dances: Samba, Cha-cha-cha, Rumba, Jive and Paso doble.

 It was 7:00 at night.

Before going to dinner, we went to the sun set in the park.

After a while, Dick leaned on me and held my right shoulder.

He held me down and kissed me on the lips.

THE END

ABOUT THE AUTHOR

Filippo Aki Pignatelli was born the 14th January 2012.

In 2018, he married Alice Orlando, but had not a single clue of how she felt.

He wrote this book in 2020.

The main idea was how his wife felt when they married.

This book is dedicated to her.

Filippo Aki Pignatelli also wrote: The Haunted House Of James, Rory The Monkey, Dog Man Petey's Escape, My grandfather Valentino, The great fire of London Series, The Haunted House Of James 2, Christmas stories, Halloween stories, Ice cream, Luna and Stella and Journey through the forest.

ACKNOLOGMENTS

I want to thank a few people for bringing this story to life. Firstly, my wife Alice Orlando for making me think the story out and how she inspired me for the characters.

Secondly, my mum who edited this book with me and my dad who started to translate this romance in Italian.

Lastly, my cat Tabby who reread it with me.

My name is Amy.

I have always wanted to marry.

Help me find the right husband with Dick,

Mum, Dad, Mary, Anna and Rover.

Printed in Great Britain
by Amazon